Happy Haunting!

Find out more spooky secrets about

Ghostville Elementary™

Ghostville Elementary™

Happy Haunting!

by **Marcia Thornton Jones**
and
Debbie Dadey

illustrated by **Jeremy Tugeau**

A
LITTLE APPLE
PAPERBACK

SCHOLASTIC INC.
New York Toronto London Auckland Sydney
Mexico City New Delhi Hong Kong Buenos Aires

No part of this publication may be reproduced in whole or in part, stored in a retrieval system, or transmitted in any form or by any means, electronic, mechanical, photocopying, recording, or otherwise, without written permission of the publisher. For information regarding permission, write to Scholastic Inc., Attention: Permissions Department, 557 Broadway, New York, NY 10012.

ISBN 0-439-42440-2

Text copyright © 2003 by Marcia Thornton Jones and Debra S. Dadey. Illustrations copyright © 2003 by Scholastic Inc. SCHOLASTIC, LITTLE APPLE, and associated logos are trademarks and/or registered trademarks of Scholastic Inc.

12   6 7 8/0

Printed in the U.S.A.   40
First printing, September 2003

To the real Beckhams—
Barbara and Lee!

— MTJ

To Miss Webb and all the fantastic
fourth and fifth graders at
Werner Elementary

— DD

Contents

THE LEGEND

Sleepy Hollow Elementary School
Online Newspaper

This Just In: Family Night Turns into Fright Night!

Breaking News: Most kids are happy to hang artwork and set out book reports for their parents on Sleepy Hollow's annual Family Night—but not Mr. Morton's third-grade class. Since their classroom already looks like something from *Little House on the Prairie,* the class decided to celebrate the festival just like kids would have in the 1800s. Rumor has it the class is doing lots of nutty things, like setting up a haunted house in the hallway! Who knows? Maybe some real ghosts will show up to crash the party . . .

Your friendly fifth-grade reporter,
Justin Thyme

1
Harvest Festival

"Stop it," Cassidy muttered under her breath.

Ozzy didn't stop. He tickled her neck and knocked her pencil onto the floor. Of course, he didn't just reach over and flick the pencil from her desk. Instead, he oozed up through the cracks in the old wooden floor like a glowing green glob of slime. He laughed the entire time.

Getting singled out by a bully was bad enough, but Ozzy wasn't an ordinary pest. He was a ghost, and that made things ten times worse. Cassidy couldn't tell her teacher. Mr. Morton didn't exactly believe in ghosts. What would he think if Cassidy told him there were at least five ghosts in their classroom and one of them was picking on her?

Cassidy still hadn't figured out why the ghosts only appeared to her and two of her friends, Jeff and Nina. And Cassidy would never understand why Ozzy liked to bother her more than anyone else.

Mr. Morton cleared his throat and looked at Cassidy. "I have an announcement," he said.

Cassidy groaned. She hoped Mr. Morton wasn't planning a huge homework assignment. She wanted to play on her computer all afternoon.

"It's time for Sleepy Hollow's annual Family Night," Mr. Morton announced.

Every year, each class at Sleepy Hollow Elementary School planned special activities and invited their families to see what they'd been learning.

"Cool," Jeff said. "Last year, our teacher let us make a movie about our class." There was one thing Jeff loved more than anything else, and that was movies.

Cassidy's other best friend Nina smiled and raised her hand. "Mr. Morton, what is our class going to do for Family Night? Could we have a soccer tournament?" Nina ate, slept, and dreamed about sports.

Mr. Morton smiled. "That's an excellent suggestion. But I had something else in mind."

Mr. Morton wiped a layer of chalk dust from his glasses onto a piece of tissue and waited. Everyone in the class squirmed.

"Since we fixed up our classroom to look like a one-room schoolhouse," Mr. Morton began, "I think we should celebrate our Family Night just as the pioneers would have celebrated a harvest festival in the 1800s."

Jeff dropped his head onto his desk with a bang. There were no video cameras or movies in the 1800s.

"And," Mr. Morton continued as he put his glasses back on, "I think you should invite your parents, grandparents, and neighbors to join the celebration."

Now it was Cassidy's turn to put her head down. She gave a big sigh and looked out a basement window. It was so foggy she couldn't see outside. Olivia, the janitor, definitely needed to clean that window. Cassidy closed her eyes and thought about her grandfather.

Her grandfather used to be fun. He'd taken her to the zoo, amusement parks, and even a weeklong trip to the beach where he taught her to bodysurf. That was before her grandmother had died and he'd moved into the spare bedroom

in Cassidy's house. Now her grandfather was grumpy and nosy. He probably wouldn't come to her school, even if she did invite him.

With her eyes closed, Cassidy could hear Jeff telling Nina about his grandparents. "They live too far away to come," he said, "but I bet my neighbor Mrs. Beckham will come. She's the same age as my grandparents."

"That's a great idea," a girl named Carla said.

Cassidy could hear Carla's twin giggling. "We could invite Mr. Woods," Darla said. "He's our neighbor. He went to this school when he was a kid."

"My *abuela* only speaks Spanish," Nina said. "But I can explain everything to her."

"Then it's settled," Mr. Morton said as other kids around the classroom nodded. "We'll invite grandparents and friends to our 1800s Harvest Festival."

Cassidy opened her eyes just in time to

see the fog on the window being swirled into a picture by an invisible hand. Cassidy recognized the picture. It was Ozzy's face, and he was sticking out his tongue at Cassidy.

2
Nosy

"It's freezing out here," Nina complained as they left school that afternoon. The three friends were on their way to Cassidy's house for a snack.

"Why don't you put on your sweater?" Jeff asked as a cool wind blew leaves all around them.

Nina shrugged and rubbed her arms. "I can't find it. I know I took it to school this

morning, but when I went to get it from the coat closet it was gone."

"Maybe it's in the same place as my new pencil," Cassidy said. "It disappeared yesterday."

"I have to find it before the festival," Nina said. "My *abuela* knitted it for me. I want to show her I like it by wearing it."

"Please don't talk about the festival at my house," Cassidy said. "I don't want my grandfather to know about it."

"Aren't you going to invite him?" Nina asked.

Cassidy shook her head. "No, he doesn't like to do fun stuff like that. Besides, he hates our school. He won't even walk by it."

"You're making that up," Jeff said.

"I don't think he wants to have anything to do with our school, so don't talk about the festival while we're in the house," Cassidy said. "My grandfather likes to listen in. He'll overhear."

When Cassidy reached for her front doorknob, the door swung right open. Her grandfather stood tall in the doorway. "How was school?" he asked. "Anything new?"

Nina opened her mouth to speak, but Cassidy answered before Nina could say a word. "Nope," Cassidy said. "Nothing new."

Cassidy's grandfather stared at her a full fifteen seconds, but Cassidy ducked by him and hurried to the kitchen. Nina and Jeff followed Cassidy.

"Do you think we could watch TV while we have our snack?" Jeff asked.

Cassidy shook her head as she pulled out a package of cookies from the pantry. "My mom won't let me watch TV until my homework is done."

"Isn't your mom at work?" Nina asked.

"Yeah," Cassidy said, "but Grandpa would tell on me. Sometimes I think he likes to get me in trouble."

"He wouldn't have to know. We could keep the volume low," Jeff said. "There's a cool rerun on this afternoon."

Cassidy shook her head and bit into a cookie. She knew her grandfather was probably just around the corner, being his usual nosy self.

"I can't believe we can't make a video for Family Night," Jeff said as he stuffed a cookie in his mouth. "It would have been so much fun."

"Shh," Cassidy warned. She wished her

friends would stop talking about the festival.

Nina wiped her mouth with a napkin. "All the grandparents will be there," she blurted out just as Cassidy's grandfather walked into the kitchen. "You have to tell your grandfather about the festival!"

3
Ghost Attack

The next day at school, Mr. Morton rubbed his hands together, and a little cloud of chalk dust formed over his head. "Today," he said, "we'll plan the Harvest Festival."

Cassidy sighed. It was bad enough that the classroom ghosts picked on her half the time. Now her teacher was going to make the class work on the festival. The last thing she wanted to think about was inviting her grandfather to school, but since Nina had spilled the beans, Cassidy didn't know how she could get out of it.

"We'll work in groups to plan activities," Mr. Morton continued.

As soon as the words were out of his mouth, the class went into action. Kids jumped out of their seats. They shouted

14

across the room. Everybody scrambled to find a partner. Mr. Morton clapped his hands for order, but no one paid any attention.

Jeff pulled Cassidy and Nina to the back of the room where they could talk without being heard.

"Hey," Andrew yelled once everyone had settled down. "Who took my cookies?" He held up an empty plastic bag.

Carla held out her hands. "What cookies? We didn't . . ."

". . . take them," added her twin sister Darla.

"Well, somebody stole them," Andrew fumed. He glanced around the room, looking for chocolate on chins.

Mr. Morton clapped his hands. "Cookies," he said, "would be a great idea for the festival. Your group can find out what kind of cookies pioneers ate in the 1800s and bake them for our guests."

Andrew's partners groaned. "That means we have to do research," a girl named Meredith complained.

"And we'll have to cook," a boy named Larry added.

"Cook?" Andrew sputtered. "That's a sissy project!"

"Your grandparents will enjoy the feeling of stepping back in time to sample an old-fashioned recipe," Mr. Morton said with a smile. "They might even be able to give you some pointers."

Now it was Cassidy's turn to groan. She didn't want her grandfather to step back into time. And she especially didn't want him to step foot into her classroom. Unfortunately, her friends Nina and Jeff didn't feel the same way.

"Our group has to come up with something really good," Nina said. "I want my *abuela* to have fun."

Jeff nodded. "My neighbor Mrs. Beckham would love to see something that reminds her of her childhood," he said. "Did you get any ideas off the Internet, Cassidy?"

Usually, Cassidy was good at coming up with plans, but this time she didn't feel like thinking. In fact, she didn't want to have anything to do with the festival. She sighed again. "We could bob for apples," she finally said.

As soon as the words were out of her

mouth, a cold wind whipped the hair back from her face. Cassidy shivered, hugging herself for warmth.

Nina's lips trembled. She pointed above Cassidy's head. "I think our ghosts are back," Nina said with a shaky voice.

The basement window had whitened with fog. Slowly, a single word was etched on the glass. "NO!" it said.

"That's Ozzy's handwriting," Cassidy noted.

"It looks like Ozzy doesn't like your idea," Jeff said. "Let's ignore him and get back to work."

Nina glanced one more time at the window. "Ozzy is right. I don't think grandparents would like bobbing for apples," she said. "It might hurt their teeth."

Jeff laughed. "If they still have any teeth. Of course, they could take out their dentures and use their hands to snap those choppers shut on the apples."

Cassidy couldn't help laughing at the thought of false teeth floating around in a tub of water.

"I have another idea." Nina grabbed a piece of paper and started sketching as she talked. "We can collect empty thread spools and tie them together to make dolls,"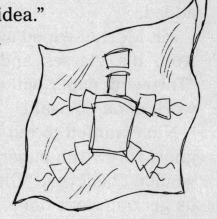

she explained. "I've seen them in pictures."

Just as Nina finished her sketch of a spool doll, the paper flew out of her fingers and wadded itself into a tight ball. Nina reached for it, but she wasn't fast enough. The wad of paper flew across the room all by itself and landed on Carla's head.

Carla waved her hand in the air to get Mr. Morton's attention. "Excuse me, Mr. Morton. Mr. Morton!" Carla said. "Nina threw paper at me."

"It landed on Carla's head," Darla added.

Mr. Morton wiped away the chalk dust from his glasses and peered at Nina. "Throwing paper will not help us get our work done," he said.

Nina wanted to tell her teacher that a ghost threw the paper, but she knew he wouldn't believe it. "Ghosts aren't helping us get our work done, either," Nina muttered so only Cassidy and Jeff could hear.

"Speaking of ghosts," Cassidy whispered. "Look!" The four kids turned to see Ozzy floating above Mr. Morton's head. Actually, Ozzy wasn't floating. He was dancing and he wasn't alone.

In the air above Mr. Morton, the whole ghost group was dancing. Becky, Sadie, Nate, Edgar, and Ozzy swung one another around and stomped in the air. Papers blew off their teacher's desk and a whole container of thumbtacks flew around the room. Kids ducked just in time to avoid getting nailed by a thumbtack.

"Yikes!" Cassidy hissed as she ducked under her desk. "Watch out for the ghostly tacks."

"You mean, the ghostly *attack*!" Jeff said as he hid behind his math book.

Thanks to his dust-covered glasses, Mr. Morton didn't seem to notice the flying tacks or the ducking kids.

"They're doing some kind of square dance!" Jeff exclaimed.

Mr. Morton looked at Jeff and smiled.

21

"Square dancing! That's a great idea. Who'd like to arrange a square dance for the festival?"

"We would!" Carla and Darla called out.

"What's with these ghosts today?" Nina asked. "Ozzy can be a stinker, but the rest of them usually let us get our work done."

Jeff snapped his fingers in front of Nina's nose. "I know why our ghosts are bothering us," he said. "Maybe they're unhappy about our grandparents and friends coming to the classroom for the Harvest Festival."

"Why would having company make ghosts unhappy?" Nina asked.

Jeff pulled his friends close. "I saw something like this in a movie once. A ghost was hiding something so terrible the camera wouldn't even show it."

"Are you trying to tell us that Ozzy and his ghost friends are hiding something in the basement?" Nina asked.

Jeff nodded. "And whatever it is, it's

something so horrible they don't want anyone to know about it."

"You're crazy," Cassidy told him. "Olivia cleans down here every day. If there was anything to be found, she would know about it."

"The ghosts probably don't understand what the Harvest Festival is about," Nina added. "If they did, they would be excited. The festival would be the perfect time for them to go into action. Haunting action."

"Shh," Jeff warned. But he was too late.

Ozzy laughed wickedly from the air behind Cassidy's head.

"What a great idea," Ozzy whispered so only the three friends could hear. "A wonderful, haunting idea!"

4
Tornado

"NO!" Jeff, Cassidy, and Nina all yelled at the same time.

Mr. Morton wiped his glasses and peered at them. "Is there a problem?" he asked.

Ozzy soared through the air to hover over Mr. Morton. Ozzy made circles with his fingers and thumbs, pretending they were glasses. He let his eyes grow to the size of balloons. "Might there be a problem?" Ozzy mocked.

Of course, Mr. Morton didn't hear him. The ghosts only allowed a few people to see and hear what they did — and none of them were adults.

"No problem," Nina said, trying to ignore Ozzy.

"None at all," Jeff added.

Cassidy wasn't looking at Mr. Morton. She was watching Ozzy instead. He had just plucked out his eyeballs and popped them in his mouth. "We were thinking about something a little scary," she admitted.

"Scary?" Carla asked.

"We don't like scary things," Darla added.

Andrew looked at the twins and pretended to shiver. "Then make sure you don't look in any mirrors," he teased.

Cassidy ignored the other kids while Ozzy popped his eyeballs back into his head. "In fact," Cassidy said, "we just came up with a great idea."

"We did?" Nina squeaked.

Cassidy nodded. "People in the 1800s told ghost stories just like we do today."

"Cassidy's right," Jeff said. "Some of my favorite movies are based on stories written in the 1800s."

"So we were thinking about making the basement hallway into a haunted house for the festival," Cassidy told Mr. Morton.

Carla gasped. Darla groaned. Andrew slapped his hand on his desk. "Now, that's what I call a great idea. Much better than baking cookies!"

Mr. Morton broke into a huge grin. "Brilliant!" he said. "You can show how traditions from today aren't completely different from long ago."

"We can?" Nina asked.

"That's exactly what we plan to do," Cassidy said with a determined nod. She totally ignored Ozzy, whose head was spinning like a top.

"Have you lost your marbles?" Nina asked once everyone else had gone back to work. Her face had grown pale and her eyes were round. "The basement is haunted enough without our help."

Cassidy patted Nina on the shoulder. "Calm down," she said. "This way, if the ghosts act up, everyone will think it was part of our plan."

Jeff tapped a pencil on the floor and grinned. "You might be on to something," he said.

"But what if the ghosts *really* act up?" Nina asked. "They could cause big trouble."

Cassidy jutted out her chin and put her hands on her hips. "Then we'll have to be ready for them," she said. "But first, let's go out in the hall and plan a Harvest Festival that no one will ever forget."

The three friends politely asked Mr. Morton to be excused. Then they slipped out into the hallway. As soon as they left the classroom, the door slammed shut and a wave of cold air blew past them. "Making this look haunted will be about as hard as getting a cat to chase mice," Jeff pointed out.

He was right. Weak sunlight struggled

through a grimy window at one end of the hall. Cobwebs clung to the damp walls above their heads. Shadows cloaked the closed doors on either side of the hall, making them look like giant black eyes. An old wooden cupboard built into the wall at the far end of the hall looked like the doorway to a nightmare.

"Maybe we can hide a tape player in that old cupboard," Jeff suggested. "We can play scary music."

He walked down the hallway and the girls followed. The farther they went from their classroom, the colder it became.

"The air feels thicker," Nina said.

"I feel like I'm walking through mud," Cassidy said.

Jeff was slowing down as he got closer to the cupboard. He leaned forward, as if he were walking into a hurricane's wind. "I can't get any closer," he said through gritted teeth. "Push me."

Nina and Cassidy shoved Jeff toward the end of the hall. Instead of going forward, Jeff bounced back against them, and all three kids tumbled to the ground.

"What's happening?" Nina cried.

"There's something in that cabinet," Cassidy said. "And I plan on finding out what it is."

As soon as the words were out of her mouth, Cassidy leaped up from the floor and jumped at the cabinet. She hooked her hands on the old wooden handle and tugged as hard as she could.

"It's stuck!" she called over her shoulder. "Help me!"

Jeff and Nina crawled toward Cassidy, but they didn't get very far. The lone window at the other end of the hall burst open and a blast of cold wind swirled dead leaves straight toward them.

"It's a tornado!" Nina screamed.

5
Haunting Help

That afternoon, Cassidy, Jeff, and Nina met at Cassidy's house to work on the decorations for their haunted hallway. They sat at the kitchen table eating Cassidy's favorite snack — peanut butter-and-jelly sandwiches with sliced bananas.

"I can't believe you thought that was a tornado," Cassidy told Nina.

"What was I supposed to think?" Nina asked. "That wind was so strong it blew open the window and dumped a ton of leaves in the hallway."

That much seemed true. When Mr. Morton saw the mess, he made the three friends clean it up.

"The wind isn't as strange as that cabinet," Jeff pointed out. "Did you notice

33

that even the leaves stayed at least three feet away from it?"

"It's almost as if the cabinet was pushing away everything that got close," Cassidy said thoughtfully, "as though it didn't want anything to get near it."

Nina licked a smudge of peanut butter off her arm before shaking her head. "A piece of furniture cannot decide what gets near it," she said.

"Maybe it's not the cabinet," Cassidy said. "Maybe it's the ghosts."

"What are you talking about?" Jeff asked.

"Ozzy is bad enough on a good day," Cassidy explained. "Lately, he's been worse than usual. I think it has something to do with the festival. That mysterious cabinet and strange wind must be part of it, too."

Jeff laughed. "We have a school basement filled with ghosts and you think wind is strange?"

"Shh," Cassidy hissed and pointed at the kitchen door. Cassidy's grandfather had paused in the hall before heading toward the den. Cassidy was sure he was listening.

"We have to be careful with my grandfather around," Cassidy warned them. "He tries to hear everything we're saying."

"Your grandfather is just interested," Nina said. "Grandparents are like that. My *abuela* likes to listen to my friends, too."

"Your grandmother only speaks Spanish. She can't understand most of what we're saying," Cassidy pointed out. "But my grandfather understands every single word. I think he spies on us."

"Let's forget about all this talk of spies and ghosts," Jeff suggested. "We have to come up with ideas for the haunted hallway. Mr. Morton said we can start putting up decorations tomorrow."

The three friends huddled around the table to make their plans. The more they talked, the more frustrated they became. Haunting a basement was harder than it sounded. "We need ghosts, spiders, and more cobwebs," Nina finally said.

"Maybe we could have a headless horseman," Jeff suggested.

"Where are we going to find those things?" Cassidy asked. "We need haunting help!"

"Maybe I could help," Cassidy's grandfather said from the shadows of the doorway.

Cassidy's face turned red as her grandfather walked into the kitchen and sat down. She didn't like it one bit that he had been listening, but her grandfather didn't seem to notice.

"We can stuff plastic garbage bags with leaves to make giant spiders," he said.

"They didn't have plastic garbage bags

back in the olden days," Cassidy pointed out.

Cassidy's grandfather nodded. "We could use black material instead. And quilters use a white flimsy material called batting. I think it would make great cobwebs if you stretched it out and attached it to the ceiling."

"That's a great idea!" Nina said. "How did you think of it?"

Cassidy's grandfather smiled, but his eyes still looked sad. "Cassidy's grandmother was a genius when it came to decorating and crafts," he explained. "She used to make all of the grandkids' Halloween costumes. She made their Christmas dresses. She painted all their Easter baskets and Easter eggs. I just happened to pick up on some of her ideas."

"I bet she knew lots of things that would help us with the festival," Jeff said.

Cassidy's grandfather nodded. "She was

smart. Cassidy takes after her grandmother. I'll show you her picture."

Cassidy's grandfather hurried to the den and came back with a thick photo album. He shoved the jars of peanut butter and jelly out of the way and placed the album on the kitchen table. Jeff and Nina huddled close to see. As he turned the pages of his wife's album, he told the kids about her. "Here are pictures from when she won the blue ribbon for quilting at the state fair," he said, pointing to a picture. "She designed the pattern herself. Her entire family was clever."

He turned another page to show them a picture of some of her relatives. Suddenly, Jeff yelped. Nina gasped.

Cassidy looked at her friends. "What's wrong?" she asked.

They pointed to the picture staring up at them from the table. It was an old picture of Sleepy Hollow Elementary School before it was rebuilt. In the picture was a

girl who looked
exactly like Cas-
sidy. The girl in the
photo was slipping a toad
down the pants of a boy they
all recognized.

Ozzy.

6
Homer

"This isn't working right," Nina told her friends the next day at school. The three kids were in the hallway trying to get the cotton batting to look like spiderwebs. No matter how they tried to stretch it, it stayed in big globs.

Cassidy groaned. "This looks more like a marshmallow than a spiderweb."

"We just need to pull it more," Jeff suggested. He pulled as hard as he could and ended up with a big wad of white cotton in his face.

Jeff stuck out his arms and walked toward Nina. "I am the ghost of . . ." Nina shrieked and covered her eyes.

Cassidy grabbed the cotton off Jeff's head. "Quit fooling around," she said. "We have to get this done."

Cassidy hadn't been very talkative since finding out her great-great-great-aunt had been in Ozzy's class and that her distant relative had been the school's biggest prankster — even worse than Ozzy.

Nina tried to tape a paper sign that read **BEWARE** on the wall, but the tape wouldn't stick. The sign slid right off the wall and floated down the hall. "You know," Nina said, "if I didn't know better, I'd think the ghosts were trying to sabotage our haunted house. I bet Ozzy picks on Cassidy so much because her great-great-great-aunt always picked on him."

Cassidy folded her arms over her chest and frowned. "I think you're exactly right," she said. "Ozzy!" she snapped. "You get out here right now."

The white cotton batting glowed green. It flew up in the air and wiggled around. "It looks like a rattlesnake," Jeff said, ducking when the green snake zoomed past him.

Cassidy reached up and grabbed the cotton. She jerked it down to the floor and put her foot on it. Ozzy appeared, but his head looked squished under Cassidy's tennis shoe. "Ouch," Ozzy said. "I was only having fun."

"So it is you who's been ruining all our decorations," Nina said.

Ozzy floated out from under Cassidy's foot and smiled. "Not just me," he said. In an instant, five more glowing green

shapes sur-
rounded the
kids — Becky,
Nate, Edgar, Sadie,
and Huxley. Huxley tried to grab the batting from under Cassidy's shoes but the
ghost dog's teeth went right through it.
Edgar finished jotting in his story journal
and slammed it shut. Cassidy couldn't help
but wonder if he was writing about her.

"Why are you messing up our haunted
hallway?" Jeff asked.

Becky opened her mouth to answer,

but before she could, the kids heard a jingling noise. Or perhaps it was a jangling noise. The ghosts disappeared as quickly as they had appeared.

Around the corner came Olivia, the school janitor. Her keys jingled where they hung from her purple overalls.

"Hello, kiddos," Olivia said with a wink. "What are you up to? Trouble, no doubt."

"We're trying to hang cobwebs in the hallway," Cassidy explained.

Olivia put her hand over her heart. "Saints preserve us. I spend all my time knocking them to the ground, and you're putting more up?"

Nina laughed and explained about the haunted house. Jeff wasn't listening to Nina. He had his eyes on Olivia's new pet. A small brown weasel sat on her shoulder. Olivia's favorite pastime was rescuing injured animals.

"Can we pet your weasel?" Jeff asked, sticking out his hand.

The weasel bared its teeth at Jeff. "No,"

Olivia said firmly. "Homer is a bit ornery. He misses his mama." Olivia winked at the kids. "You know that goes for people, too. Missing someone can make anyone a bit grumpy."

"Olivia," Nina asked. "I've been wondering what's in that cabinet. Do you know?" Nina pointed to the wooden cabinet that the kids hadn't been able to open.

Olivia put her finger to her lips and her eyes flashed. She didn't yell, but the kids could tell she meant business. Something about the way Olivia spoke sent shivers up and down Nina's back. "You'd best be leaving that place alone," Olivia said, "if you know what's good for you."

7
Special Effects

Mr. Morton poked his head out the classroom door for a second. "You'll have to stop decorating now. It's time for music class."

Jeff tossed the cotton batting into a corner of the hallway and grinned. Music was one of his favorite subjects.

Cassidy frowned. She put the tape and scissors beside the wall. "We have got to think about the ghosts," she said.

Nina shook her head. "I try *not* to think about them."

"We have to come up with a plan," Cassidy reminded Nina. "What if the ghosts go crazy during the festival?"

Jeff shrugged. "We could tell our guests it was special effects, like in a movie."

"That might work," Nina said. "They do amazing things in movies."

Jeff grinned. Maybe there was a way to get movies involved in Family Night after all.

"Let's go, class," Mr. Morton said. He came out of the classroom and led the rest of the students down the hall.

Nina's mind was still on the cabinet. As the three kids filed to the end of the line, she whispered to her friends, "Now I'm really curious about that cabinet."

Jeff laughed and teased Nina, "There are probably dead bodies in there."

Nina gasped, but Cassidy frowned at Jeff. "You watch way too many scary movies," Cassidy told him. "I bet that cabinet is just full of poisonous cleaning supplies and that's why Olivia keeps it locked."

"Maybe," Jeff said with a grin, "it's . . . the poison that Olivia uses on kids she doesn't like."

Nina shivered as her class went up the stairs to the main floor of the school. She knew Jeff was just kidding, but she couldn't help wondering about Olivia. She had looked scary when she warned them to stay away from the cabinet. Still, Olivia had always been nice to them before, and she always helped animals. Maybe Cassidy was right about the cleaning supplies.

Nina sighed. She was silly to be scared of an old cabinet. She decided she had to be braver. But just then something happened to make her forget about being brave. A huge skeleton leaped in front of her. Nina did what anybody would do, brave or otherwise. She screamed.

8
Ghost-Be-Gone

"You jumped so high I'm surprised you don't have cobwebs stuck in your hair," Jeff said with a laugh.

It was the next day, and Cassidy, Nina, and Jeff were on their way to school.

"Scaring your friends is not funny," Nina said. She scratched the top of her head to make sure there weren't any cobwebs in her hair.

"Nina is right," Cassidy told Jeff. "It wasn't very nice, even if it was funny."

"That skeleton is perfect for our haunted house," Jeff argued. "I had to test it out."

Cassidy groaned. "I can't believe the festival is tonight. We're not ready."

"We'll be ready," Nina said. "Olivia helped us hang the cobwebs and giant spiders. What else do we have to do?"

"We have to make sure the *real* ghosts don't ruin our haunted basement," Cassidy said.

Nina pulled her jacket tight against the early morning chill. "If we knew how to do that, our problems would be over forever."

Jeff nodded. "Nina is right. There is no way to de-ghost our basement."

Cassidy pulled her friends into the shadows of an old weeping willow tree. "I think you're wrong," she said.

"Did you find a way to rid our school of ghosts on the Internet?" Nina asked.

It was a good question, since Cassidy spent all her free time surfing the Web, but Cassidy shook her head. "Nope, not on the Internet, in the laundry room!"

Jeff pretended to knock on Cassidy's head. "Hello?" he called. "Is anybody in there?"

Cassidy pulled away. "This is serious," she said.

"I know," Jeff said. "You're seriously

nuts. What do you plan to do? Put Ozzy
and his ghost pals in the spin cycle along
with your dirty underwear?"

Cassidy shook her head. "My grandfather made me fold the clean clothes last
night," she explained, "and the socks were
full of static electricity. It made my hair
stand straight up in the air. Grandpa
laughed. He said it happened because he
forgot to put a dryer sheet in with the
clothes. That's when I figured out the answer to all our problems!"

Jeff held out his hand to stop Cassidy's rush of words. "What in the world do socks have to do with ghosts?" he asked.

"Not the socks," Cassidy said. "The electricity! Don't you get it? What are ghosts made of?"

Jeff squared his shoulders. He knew everything there was to know about ghosts. "Ectoplasm," he said.

"And what's ectoplasm?" Cassidy asked.

"A type of energy," he said slowly.

"Bingo!" Cassidy called out. "Ghosts are built-up bundles of energy. They're like static electricity. All we have to do is get rid of their static and our problems are gone! Gone I tell you!"

"And how do we get rid of ghost static?" Nina asked.

"With my new invention," Cassidy said. She plopped her book bag on the ground and dug into the bottom. Then she pulled out a wad of dryer sheets that had been stapled together to form a curtain the size of a small blanket. "This is

my new and improved Ghost-Be-Gone
curtain. All we do is hold it up in front of
rampaging ghosts. The dryer sheets will
take away the ghosts' energy and they'll
be too tired to bother us!"

Cassidy beamed at her friends.

"Do you think it will work?" Nina asked.

"We'll find out," Cassidy said, "tonight!"

9
Sixth Sense

Cassidy was going to be late for the Harvest Festival and it was all her grandfather's fault. He was taking his time walking behind her. She stopped for the umpteenth time and turned to face her grandfather. "We're going to be late," she told him again. She knew she didn't sound very nice, but she had to be on time in case the basement ghosts started acting up. She was still mad at her parents for being out of town and unable to come to the festival.

"I'm making these old bones go as fast as I can," her grandfather told her for the umpteenth-plus-one time. "Don't worry. You won't miss much if we're a few minutes late."

Jeff and Nina were already waiting

when Cassidy and her grandfather made their way past the swing sets of Sleepy Hollow Elementary School. In fact, lots of kids were huddled on the playground while their grandparents, families, and friends got to know one another.

Jeff introduced Mrs. Beckham, and Nina introduced her grandmother. "How do you do?" Mrs. Beckham asked. She was even taller than Cassidy's grandfather and towered over Nina's *abuela.*

"*Buenas noches,*" Nina's grandmother said. She was from Mexico and spoke very little English.

Cassidy's grandfather didn't pay attention to her friends at all. Instead, he stared at the steps that led down to the basement. "Your room is down there?" he asked softly.

Cassidy nodded. "We have our own escape route to the playground," she explained. "But we'll use the inside entrance tonight so you can see how we decorated the hallway to look like a haunted house."

Cassidy's grandfather's face paled. "Maybe those decorations weren't such a good idea," he said. "This place is scary enough without them."

Cassidy guided her grandfather toward the school. "It's not that scary," she said. "I'll show you."

She led her grandfather into the front doors of the school. Nina and Jeff followed. Mrs. Beckham was so busy asking Nina's *abuela* how to say everything in Spanish that they fell farther and farther behind.

When Cassidy reached the top of the basement steps, her grandfather paused. "It's cold," he said with a shiver. "Very cold. There's something wrong here. I feel it in my bones."

Nina pulled Cassidy and Jeff aside. "Do you think your grandfather knows about the ghosts?" Nina whispered.

"No," Cassidy told her. "He would have said something to my parents before now if he did."

Jeff grabbed Cassidy's arms. "I know what's happening. Your grandfather must have some sort of sixth sense."

"What are you taking about?" Nina asked. "There are only five senses. We learned them in kindergarten." She ticked them off on her fingers. "Sight, hearing, taste, smell, and touch."

Jeff shook his head. "Some people can sense when things aren't right. They can just feel it. It's called a sixth sense."

The kids stared at Cassidy's grandfather. He stood at the top of the basement stairs with a horrible look on his face. Cassidy gulped. "He knows what's down there."

"We have nothing to worry about," Nina said in a shaky voice. "The ghosts have never shown themselves to adults."

Cassidy nodded. "Not yet." She took a deep breath. "Now, let's get this over with." Cassidy walked back to her grandfather and took his elbow. "There's nothing to worry about," she told him. She just hoped she was telling the truth.

Slowly, the four made their way down the steps. As soon as they entered the basement, Cassidy's grandfather broke into a huge grin. "The cobwebs and giant spiders look great," he said. "Your grandmother couldn't have done a better job!"

Cassidy couldn't help smiling and feeling a little proud.

Jeff quickly opened the door to their classroom and punched a button on a tape player. Immediately, strains of haunting music floated through the air.

"This room looks like classrooms did when I went to school," Cassidy's grandfather said when he walked into their classroom. He seemed much happier as he looked at the old pictures hanging on the wall. When he saw the wood-burning stove he laughed out loud. "When I was a little boy, I came to school early in the morning to start the stove for my teacher," he said. "It was very much like this one. In exchange, my teacher gave me candy for Christmas. It was the only candy I got all year."

"You mean, you had to work for candy?" Jeff said. "That's unbelievable!"

"It's true!" a voice suddenly echoed.

Cassidy's grandfather turned on his heels to face the new voice. When he did, his face turned as white as a cloud and he fainted straightaway.

10
Grandpa

"Grandpa," Cassidy screamed. She fell beside her grandfather and patted his face. Her grandfather was breathing, but he didn't move. Cassidy couldn't stand it. Nina and Jeff gathered around Cassidy and her grandfather.

"Please, Grandpa, please be okay," Cassidy pleaded. "I'm sorry I've been so mean to you lately. Please wake up."

Grandfather's eyelashes flickered and Cassidy held her breath. Slowly, he opened his eyes. "Where are my glasses?" he asked.

"We'll find them," Cas- sidy assured

him. Jeff, Cassidy, and Nina looked all around the classroom.

"I don't see them anywhere," Cassidy said, bending over to check under nearby desks.

"I bet the ghosts hid them," Nina whispered to Cassidy.

"Those ghosts are in big trouble," Cassidy said.

"Oh, no," Jeff gasped. "They're going to ruin the festival."

"You mean our freaky festival," Nina said with a gulp. The three kids stared as Ozzy, Becky, Sadie, and Nate flew around the room. They juggled the spools from the doll-making station and splashed water from the apple-bobbing area. Huxley, their ghost dog, jumped from ghost to ghost, trying to grab things as they flew through the air. Edgar hovered above Mr. Morton's desk with his journal and pencil. He wrote down everything his ghost buddies did.

"Those ghosts are going to regret

messing with me," Cassidy said, putting her hands on her hips.

"Cassidy?" her grandfather called. "Have you found my glasses yet?"

Cassidy ran over to her grandfather. "Not yet, Grandpa. I'll find them," she promised.

Her grandfather took Cassidy's hand. "Something is wrong with your classroom," he told her. "All my life I've been able to sense things, even when I was a boy at Sleepy Hollow Elementary."

Cassidy looked at her grandfather. He looked scared and sad all at the same time. She remembered the times, the old times, when he was happy all the time. Suddenly, Cassidy was very glad her grandfather was there. "I know," she said. "I feel it, too."

Her grandfather looked at her in surprise. "You do?"

"But don't worry," Cassidy told him. "Everything will be all right. I know exactly what to do."

Cassidy, Nina, and Jeff ran into the hallway, away from all the decorations and people. "You'd better get out of here right away, Ozzy!" Cassidy told the ghost.

Five glowing green forms hovered in the air beside the kids. The forms sparkled and wavered. Finally, six ghosts materialized: Ozzy, Nate, Becky, Edgar, Sadie, and Huxley.

Ozzy blew a fog of green ectoplasm in Cassidy's face. "You don't tell us what to do," Ozzy told Cassidy.

"You sound just like that horrible girl

Lucy," Becky said. She stuck out her lower lip and kicked at a chair. "She was always trying to tell us what to do, too."

Nina leaned over and whispered in Cassidy's ear. "She must be talking about your great-great-great-aunt."

"This has nothing to do with my Great-Aunt Lucy," Cassidy said to the ghosts. "It's about what *you* did. You made my grandfather faint," Cassidy said, unzipping her backpack to pull out her Ghost-Be-Gone curtain, "and that means you're history."

11
Ghost Hugs

Before Cassidy could take out the curtain, Becky started crying.

"What's wrong?" Nina asked.

Huge sobs wracked Becky's body. Ghostly wails filled the hallway.

"Shh," Jeff said. "Everything will be all right."

Ozzy shook his head. "All this talk of grandparents has Becky missing ours. Grandma and Grandpa Martin raised us."

"They spoiled them rotten," Sadie added, and Becky cried even harder. Teardrops dribbled off her chin and plopped to the floor. Cassidy noticed a huge puddle forming around Becky's feet.

"And Cassidy's Great-Great-Great-Aunt Lucy made fun of them for being so spoiled," Edgar added.

"I want Grandma and Grandpa," Becky wailed.

"Now you see why we tried to keep the grandparents from coming to the festival," Nate said.

"And we didn't want you to find . . ." Sadie started to say.

"Shh," Ozzy hissed.

"Your grandpa looks like mine," Becky moaned.

Cassidy couldn't help feeling sorry for Becky, so the Ghost-Be-Gone trap stayed in her backpack. "You have to give my grandfather back his glasses," she said. "It was mean of you to take them. He can't see very well without them."

Ozzy sighed. When he did, he seemed to deflate like an old balloon. Then he floated over to the hallway cabinet.

Nina held her breath as Ozzy oozed through the cracks of the cabinet doors and popped them open. Ozzy pulled out Nina's missing sweater. "Hey, that's

mine," she said. "You shouldn't have taken that. My *abuela* made that for me."

Becky sobbed loudly. "My grandma knit sweaters for me, too."

Ozzy handed out Cassidy's missing pencil and Andrew's cookies. Finally, her grandfather's glasses floated in the air.

"These are just like my grandpa's," Ozzy explained before slamming the cabinet shut. "And Grandma used to make cookies and help us with our homework. She made sure our pencils were sharp."

"I miss their hugs the most," Becky said between hiccups. Cassidy, Nina, and Jeff were getting a little teary-eyed. Suddenly, Cassidy had a great idea.

"Hurry," she told the ghosts. "Follow me." Cassidy rushed into the classroom and handed her grandfather his glasses.

"Grandpa, will you give me a hug? No questions asked?" asked Cassidy.

Her grandfather opened his mouth to ask a question, but then he nodded. He opened his arms wide. Cassidy looked at Ozzy and Becky. "Now, let's hug."

Becky had tears running down her face. Even Ozzy's eyes looked a little teary. Together, Cassidy, Ozzy, and Becky hugged Cassidy's grandfather all at the same time.

Cassidy's grandfather felt a cold draft, but as he hugged his only granddaughter there was so much warmth it didn't matter. Cassidy smiled up at him.

"Everyone needs a hug now and then," Jeff whispered to Nina. "Even a ghost."

The Harvest Festival was a big success. Everyone had so much fun that nobody, except Cassidy, noticed shaky letters appearing on the foggy window. They spelled out, THANK YOU.

Cassidy smiled. If Mr. Morton hadn't been there, she would've been tempted to thank Ozzy and the rest of the ghosts for helping her realize how important grandparents can be.

In a second, the words faded away. A picture of a girl with a frog on her head appeared. The smile faded from Cassidy's face and she shivered. She knew that Ghostville Elementary's haunted days were far from over. In fact, they had just begun.

Ready for more spooky fun?
Then take a sneak peek at the next

Ghostville Elementary™

#5 Stage Fright

Finally, at two o'clock in the afternoon, Mr. Morton cleared his throat. "Okay, class," he announced. "It's time for the play auditions."

A few kids groaned, but most kids cheered. Carla and Darla clapped their hands. Everyone put away their spelling worksheets and took out their copy of the book the class had been reading to-gether.

"Remember, each part is important," Mr. Morton told the class. "And we will need many students to make the set and decorations for the play."

"Now, let's see who is interested in playing Travis?" Mr. Morton asked. Jeff, Andrew, and Cassidy raised their hands in the air.

Jeff looked at Andrew. "I thought you didn't like plays," Jeff said.

Andrew shrugged. "I thought I'd give it a try."

Andrew went first. Jeff had to admit that Andrew was pretty good. Cassidy went next and read her part out loud. Jeff sank down in his seat. Cassidy was really good, too.

When Mr. Morton called his name, Jeff walked slowly to the front of the room. Jeff turned his book to page six and opened his mouth. Nothing came out.

Jeff stood frozen to the floor like time had stopped.

"What's wrong with Jeff?" Nina whispered to Cassidy.

Cassidy didn't say anything, either. She just pointed. When Nina saw what Cassidy was pointing at, Nina froze, too. . . .

Jeff stared at a strange figure hovering in the back corner of the room. It was a girl dressed in a flowing white gown. Her long dark hair floated above her head as she bowed slightly at Jeff.

Of course, only Jeff, Cassidy, and Nina could see her. The rest of the class, including their teacher, didn't realize a new ghost was in their midst.

"Jeff? Jeff?" Mr. Morton asked. "Are you okay?"

Jeff's mouth moved, but no sound came out.

"Look at him," Andrew blurted. "He's got stage fright."

"It's a fright, all right," Nina murmured. "But it has nothing to do with a stage."

The new ghost slowly floated through the air, straight to the items the kids had brought back from the Blackburn Estate. Her slender pale finger ran along the chip on the small dish. Finally, the strange ghost paused in front of the fiddle and smiled. She gently plucked three strings. They played the same tune Cassidy had heard when they left the Blackburn Estate. The notes seemed to bounce off the walls as the ghost floated over to stand beside Jeff. The ghost tilted her head, closed her eyes, and began to sing.

Her voice was high and loud. A good dose of screeching was mixed in, though it sounded like it came from a different part of the room. . . .

Nina put her fingers in her ears. Cassidy covered her ears with her hands. Jeff stood at the front of the room and stared.

Of course, they were the only kids who saw or heard any of the ghostly antics.

"Don't you want to try out for the play?" Mr. Morton asked Jeff gently. "You don't have to if you don't want to. I can give the part to someone else."

That was enough to snap Jeff out of his stupor. He forgot all about ghosts and looked at his teacher. "Of course I want to try out," he said. "I'm perfect for this part."

Jeff tried to ignore the singing. . . . He concentrated on reading the lines for the play. "Arliss, you get out of that water," he began reading.

But the louder the new ghost sang, the louder Jeff had to yell out his part. Soon, he was shouting so loudly the kids in the front row had to cover their ears. Carla and Darla giggled and Andrew laughed out loud.

"Thank you, Jeff," Mr. Morton finally said. "I think you've showed the rest of the class that you can project your voice so all can hear."

Jeff hung his head and walked back to his seat.

Just then Huxley, the ghost dog, appeared in the middle of the room and lifted his nose toward the bookshelves. He let out a howl that Cassidy was sure shook the walls. It was so loud, in fact, that it broke the ghost sound barrier. Everyone in the class could hear the ghostly howl. Mr. Morton stopped dead in his tracks. Carla and Darla screamed. Andrew fell to the ground and hid under his desk.

Mr. Morton wiped at his glasses until he had two clear circles to see through. "What was that?" Mr. Morton gasped.

The room had suddenly grown quiet — very quiet. Cassidy, Nina, and Jeff looked around. That's when Jeff saw a tiny shadow huddled on the bookshelves.

"Oh, no," he muttered. "It can't be!"

About the Authors

Marcia Thornton Jones and Debbie Dadey got into the *spirit* of writing when they worked together at the same school in Lexington, Kentucky. Since then, Debbie has *haunted* several states. She currently *haunts* Ft. Collins, CO, with her three children, two dogs, and husband. Marcia remains in Lexington, KY, where she lives with her husband and two cats. Debbie and Marcia have fun with spooky stories. They have scared themselves silly with *The Adventures of the Bailey School Kids* and *The Bailey City Monsters* series.

MEET
Geronimo Stilton

A REPORTER WITH A NOSE FOR GREAT STORIES

Who is Geronimo Stilton? Why, that's me! I run a newspaper, but my true passion is writing tales of adventure. Here on Mouse Island, my books are all bestsellers! What's that? You've never read one? Well, my books are full of fun. They are whisker-licking-good stories, and that's a promise!

www.scholastic.com/kids

SCHOLASTIC

GERSTT

MORE SERIES YOU'LL LOVE